Disney
Z-O-M-B-I-E-S
WELCOME TO
SEABROOK

Adapted by **Bonnie Steele**

Based on the **Disney Original Movies** by **David Light and Joseph Raso**

Disney PRESS
Los Angeles • New York

Printed in the United States of America
First Paperback Edition, July 2022
ISBN 978-1-368-07322-6
FAC-029261-22154

For more Disney Press fun, visit www.disneybooks.com.

SUSTAINABLE
FORESTRY
INITIATIVE
Certified Sourcing
www.sfiprogram.org
SFI-01415

SEABROOK UNITED!

ZED Take a walk down any street in Seabrook and you might see a group of humans heading to the high school to cheer on Seabrook's awesome football team . . . zombies ordering **cauli-brains** fro-yo from a vendor cart . . . or a pack of werewolves howling as they admire the latest fashions in shop windows. This charming town is a welcoming community where everyone lives together in harmony. It's strong, united, and **tight-knit**, but it hasn't always been that way.

ADDISON With its sparkling blue coastline and lush green forests, Seabrook may be picture-perfect, but it's also a hotbed of supernatural activity. Two hundred years ago, my ancestors chased werewolves deep into the forests and stole their most precious resource—**the moonstone**. Undeterred, the werewolves made their own community in the Forbidden Forest, forging a home of their own.

Those first settlers harvested the industrial-strength moonstone power at **Seabrook Power Plant**, and Seabrook thrived. As the town prospered, its residents started to build perfect homes on uniform streets. Everyone wanted to **fit in**, so they dressed in neat, perfect outfits. To preserve this perfect lifestyle, Seabrook residents became wary of outsiders. They didn't want anyone to mess with the status quo.

Years later, an alien scout ship looking for a new planet for its people to call home landed—or should we say **"crashed"**?—in Seabrook. The young scout had run out of gas, and when her spaceship plummeted to the ground, she was seriously hurt. She could have died from her injuries, but she was discovered by a local boy named Eli, who hid the young alien and nursed her back to health.

The otherworldly visitor couldn't get in contact with her people, so her once vibrant blue hair faded to white, and she lost her alien stardust sparkle. But she wasn't alone. She and Eli fell in love, and Seabrook became her new home. Here she was able to live undetected among the other residents. She went to Seabrook High and discovered cheerleading, which became her passion. It was about the same time that the Mighty Shrimp cheer squad began its championship reign. While the cheer squad was pretty amazing, Seabrook High's football team had some catching up to do.

 Fast-forward to just fifty years ago, when a terrible accident occurred at the Seabrook Power Plant. A worker spilled his **lime soda** on a power board, creating a contaminated green haze that blew west and turned everyone in its path into dead-eyed brain-eating zombies. Those were dark times for Seabrook.

NOTHING BUT LOVE FOR YOU!

ADDISON

After the zombie apocalypse, Seabrook built a barrier to keep its residents safe from the zombie hordes. The plan was for zombies to reside in Zombietown, away from the safe streets of Seabrook. Zombies were to follow a strict set of anti-monster laws, including a curfew and government-mandated clothing, and Seabrook residents could return to their perfect lives. We didn't really understand what it was like for the zombies on the other side of the wall.

Seabrook grew even warier of outsiders and started to dislike anyone or anything that was different. No one wanted to stand out, so everyone did their best to fit in. Making the **cheer squad** was one way you could comfortably blend into the Seabrook community. Being a member of the award-winning squad brought instant acceptance.

On the other side of the wall, the zombies had some good news. The **Z-Band** was invented, and this powerful device helped zombies maintain a calm demeanor. Zombietown evolved into a warm, welcoming community, where zombies raised families, took pride in their homes, and even gathered for dance parties at the deserted Seabrook Power Plant, which had been closed down indefinitely since the accident.

Eventually, Seabrook began to loosen the zombie rules. Zombies were even invited to attend high school with the humans at Seabrook High. For many of the human and zombie teens, it was the first time the two groups had interacted. The humans had heard stories from their parents about what zombies were like, but they didn't have firsthand experience. I had never met a zombie until I met Zed, and he definitely wasn't what I had expected.

Zombies were sent to the basement when we first arrived at Seabrook High, and it was pretty obvious that some kids were afraid of us. But once they got to know us and see that we weren't that different from them, we started to really fit in.

Then, just when life in Seabrook was settling into a comfortable groove, the werewolves arrived. The pack had begun feeling their powers drain from their moonstone necklaces, so they came out of the forest to search for their legendary moonstone to recharge. Since their home in the Forbidden Forest was in the Seabrook school district, they even decided to attend Seabrook High.

Luckily, with Addison's help, we were all able to come together to uncover the location of the moonstone. The werewolves were able to recharge their moonstone necklaces, and they regained their powers. Today the moonstone can be found in the heart of Zombietown on Moonstone Circle.

With zombies, werewolves, and humans all living together in harmony, Seabrook finally accepted that anybody residing in the town belonged here. The town council did away with their anti-monster laws, and the barriers between Zombietown and Seabrook came down.

Then, one night, before the big championship game, aliens arrived in Seabrook to search for their scout ship that had crashed in the town years earlier. They were on a quest to find the log of the original scout, who had been looking for a new home for their people. She said she had hidden the map to that location in the most precious thing in Seabrook, and eventually the aliens discovered what that precious thing was.

Today humans, aliens, zombies, and werewolves celebrate under a banner declaring one hundred years of Seabrook. What will the next hundred years hold for this monster-friendly town? Only time will tell. . . .

SEABROOK MAP

RIVERBROOK ESTATES

WEREWOLF LAIR

BROOKLANE GLEN

BROOKSIDE HEIGHTS

SEARIDGE POINT

BROOK BOROUGH

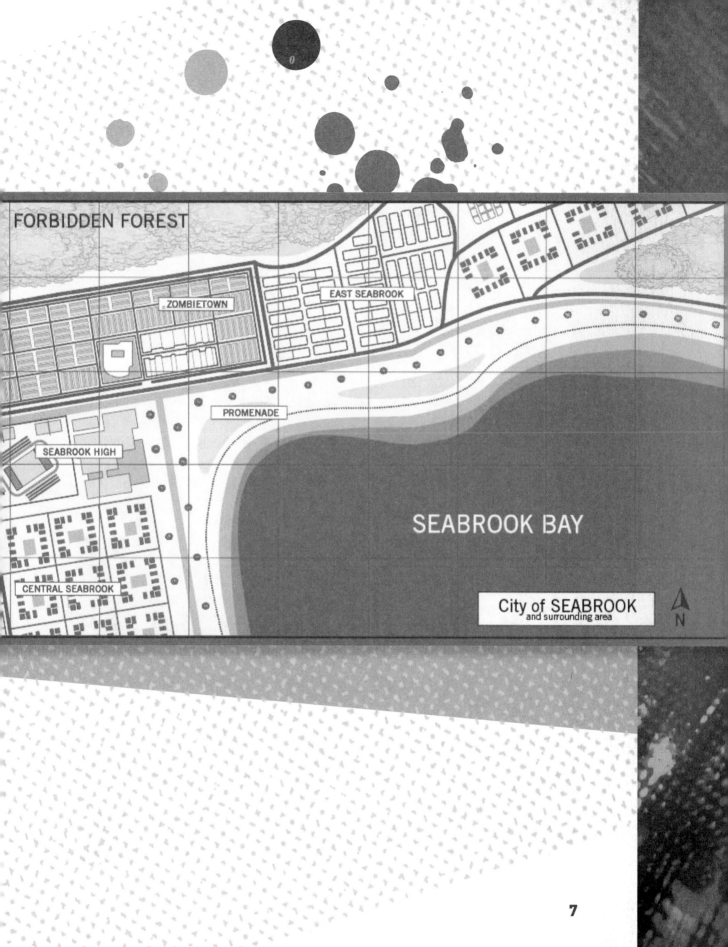

FORBIDDEN FOREST

ZOMBIETOWN

EAST SEABROOK

PROMENADE

SEABROOK HIGH

SEABROOK BAY

CENTRAL SEABROOK

City of SEABROOK
and surrounding area

N

KEEP CALM AND ZOMBIE ON!

ADDISON There was a time when people were afraid of zombies. One look at their green hair and pale skin, and Seabrook humans would run away in **fear**. According to Seabrook history, zombies even tried to eat my grandfather. Luckily, he escaped, but not without losing an ear.

After the zombie outbreak, Seabrook residents and zombies had to find a way to **coexist**, so Seabrook built a giant barrier to keep zombies out. Zombies were relegated to Zombietown, where they could lead peaceful lives with other zombies if they followed Seabrook's **anti-monster laws**. Zombies had to dress according to Seabrook laws, be home by curfew, and even shop in certain stores. Their rights were limited, but in time, Seabrook's anti-monster laws just became a **way of life**.

Eventually, after the invention of the **Z-Band**, Seabrook loosened anti-zombie measures. When my friends and I were allowed to attend Seabrook High, we didn't know what to expect from this first attempt at integration. **Change takes time.** I think that change started when I became the first zombie to play for the Seabrook High football team. It got zombiekind noticed, and people started to realize zombies are **awesome**!

Z-BANDS ZAP OUT ZOMBIE IMPULSES

Science found a way to deal with zombies when a company named Z-Tech invented the **Z-Band**. The high-tech device, worn 24/7 around the wrist, delivers soothing **electromagnetic pulses** that keep zombies from zombie-ing out.

Our craving for **human brains** was gone. Instead, zombies dined on cauli-brains and even fro-yo. Bulging eyes and protruding veins also became a thing of the past for the zombie population. Today we are **calm** and even **mellow** with the help of the Z-Band.

One note of caution, though: Z-Bands can slip off-line if they are accidentally banged hard or are affected by a computer glitch. In such cases, zombies can return to their natural state. Seabrook has taken precautionary measures for such cases. The **Z-Patrol** is a special division of the Seabrook Police Department, with officers trained to deal with random zombie incidents. Around town and in the schools, Z-Safe Rooms are available for Seabrook residents to take refuge in the case of a **Z-Alert**.

While the Z-Band keeps zombies from being, well, zombies, not all of our zom-traits are gone. Some zombies are still afraid of **fire**, and others continue to walk with a bit of a **draggy leg**, but we have come a long way since the early days of the Seabrook Power Plant incident. And Z-Tech is continuing to develop new technology for zombies.

Zombies can come to and go from **Zombietown** whenever we want today, but it hasn't always been that way. We used to have to adhere to a strict list of rules. We couldn't even own pets, because people thought that we might **eat them**!

ZOMBIE RULES

1. Wear government-issued coveralls

2. No pets

3. Follow zombie curfew

4. Stay in Zombietown unless otherwise noted

5. Wear your Z-Band at all times

DO IT LIKE THE ZOMBIES DO!

Zombies have their own **cool style**. Even back when anti-monster laws required us to wear government-issued coveralls, we knew how to swag them out. An embellished pocket, retro buttons, and even a patch or two made for individualized outfits that expressed our **zom-tastic style**.

A ZOMBIE LANDMARK

After the lime soda incident at the Seabrook Power Plant, the partially destroyed facility was closed and sat dormant in Zombietown. But we didn't let the giant empty space go to waste. After all, it had great acoustics, making it the perfect place for **zombie mash parties**. With lots of dance floor space and room for a DJ booth, Seabrook Power Plant was a cool place to hang out.

The deserted power plant also housed a **zombie light garden**. Lit by a series of single bulbs, the indoor space was a great spot to enjoy some quiet time. My little sister, Zoey, used to like to practice her cheer moves there. And the first time Addison came to Zombietown, I took her there for a little romantic stroll (after the zombie mash dance party, of course).

When Seabrook decided to **demolish the power plant** to make space for town improvements, like a cheer pavilion for its champion cheer squad, it seemed like most people thought it was time. Many zombies saw the space as an unpleasant memory of darker days. But my **zom-girl, Eliza,** wasn't too thrilled. She felt it was an important part of zombie history and should be preserved as a historical monument.

My dad was hired as foreman of the demo crew, and worked closely with Seabrook city officials to ensure the safe destruction of the empty plant. Just before the demolition was set to begin, the **werewolves** realized that the facility might be the home of their precious moonstone. They had been searching for it, and it seemed possible that this powerful energy source might be housed somewhere in the old building. Unfortunately, it was too late for the werewolves to stop the demolition, and they feared their **moonstone** had been lost forever in the explosions. (Good news: it wasn't.)

EVERYONE IS WELCOME IN ZOMBIETOWN!

ADDISON Today zombies have been fully integrated into the Seabrook community. They are artists, athletes, activists, and more! Seabrook High even just had its first **zombie valedictorian**.

The gates of Zombietown no longer serve to keep zombies out of Seabrook. Instead, they welcome everyone to this vibrant neighborhood. In fact, they've been renamed the **Unification Gates**.

Zombietown not only is home to Seabrook's zombie population, but also is where the once-thought-lost moonstone permanently resides, ensuring werewolves feel partial ownership of the neighborhood. Protected by a shimmering force field, the moonstone sits in the center of **Moonstone Circle** and is on view for all to see.

After the demolition of the Seabrook Power Plant, the town built the beautiful Seabrook **Cheer Pavilion** to honor our championship squad and give them a place to train. It also hosts cheer competitions throughout the year. As captain of the cheer squad, I planned for Seabrook to host the **National Cheer-Off** at the state-of-the-art center. Who would have thought that the competition might include alien cheerleaders from another world?

MEET ZED

- Football star
- Leader of the zombies
- First zombie to attend college

"IN SEABROOK, HUMANS, ZOMBIES, AND WEREWOLVES ARE ALL ON THE SAME TEAM."

20

I'd always dreamed of playing football when I was growing up in Zombietown, so when zombies were invited to attend Seabrook High, I couldn't wait to try out for the team. My dad was worried that I would be disappointed. "You haven't spent a whole lot of time around humans, and they don't really like zombies," he told me. **But nothing could deter me.** Even when I found out on my first day of school that zombies weren't allowed to try out for the team, I decided to go to tryouts anyway.

I didn't make the first cut—purely because I was a zombie! But when Coach saw me knock down a line of players at the pep rally to reach Addison before she fell to the ground in a cheerleading accident, he couldn't believe **my zombie strength**. What he didn't realize was that I had accidentally knocked off my Z-Band and was starting to zombie out. Coach was so excited about the possibility of me joining the team that he got Principal Lee to make an exception and let me play football.

"With a monster player like you, we can turn this team around," Coach told me. I could tell I had a little bargaining power, so I took the opportunity to ask Principal Lee for full integration of all zombies if I joined the team. **Go big or go home, right?** In good faith, she allowed the zombies to eat in the cafeteria.

At my first game, I realized I was gonna need that burst of **zombie strength** to really make a difference on the team. I asked Eliza to help me mess with my Z-Band. "If I don't win, zombies will never be accepted," I told her. "But if I win, it's a win for all of us, and we really need a win."

Eliza agreed, against her better judgment, and she got on her computer and figured out how to hack my Z-Band. We just tweaked my Z-Band at games, and I could tackle, block, and run down the field extra fast. I went on to lead the Mighty Shrimp to their first championship season ever.

A GIRL AND A ZOMBIE

I love football, but it isn't my only focus. On my first day at Seabrook High, I met a cheerleader named Addison, and—what can I say?—**I was immediately smitten**.

Addison had never met a zombie before, but I won her over with my charm. We were two freshmen from different worlds, and inhabitants of those worlds weren't really supposed to talk, let alone date. But we both felt a **connection** and didn't give up on the idea of being together. Someday maybe this could be ordinary. . . .

In the beginning, we found ways to hang out together under the radar. She cheered for me on the football field (and even left me glitter bombs in my locker). I invited her to Zombietown and later to the Prawn dance. Eventually, it didn't seem that weird for the two of us to be boyfriend and girlfriend.

LOVE

ZED FOR PRESIDENT

Even though I was **crushing it** on the football team, I decided I also wanted to have a say in school politics. Mostly, I just wanted to figure out how to make it possible for zombies to go to Prawn so I could take Addison to the dance. I decided to run for **school president**.

Eliza was the first to join my campaign team. She thought my becoming president would be a **win for the zombies**. I came up with a catchy campaign slogan: "I will bring you **prosperity** and awesomeness. I'm a zombie, not a zom-*can't*-be!" But a winning slogan doesn't mean you are going to win the election.

Unfortunately, Bucky also had his sights set on being the school president. After I accidentally zombied out while delivering my campaign platform, my presidential hopes were pretty much crushed.

A ZOMBIE GOES TO COLLEGE

When we finally got to senior year, Addison and I started to plan for a future together at Mountain College. She had already been accepted, so I just needed to become the first zombie to get into college. I was excited (and nervous) when the Mountain College recruiter came to watch me play in the championship game. Unfortunately, that game never happened, because that was the night **aliens arrived** in Seabrook.

I thought I had an impressive college application. I did well in school. In fact, my GPA was ranked third in the senior class . . . until the aliens arrived at Seabrook High. The super-smart new students from outer space quickly rose to the top of the best students list. But I **struck a deal** with them to help a zombie out. I would make sure they found what they were looking for in Seabrook, and they would help me with my college application. "The universe sent me an intergalactic alien dream team to help this zombie get into college!" I told them.

I felt like zombiekind was depending on me to get into college. Everyone really rallied together to support me when the college recruiter came to talk to me. And in the end, I got in!

MEET ELIZA

- Zed's best friend
- Hacktivist/zombie social justice warrior
- Smartest girl in school

"ZOMBIES NEED TO RISE UP. YOU WANT JUSTICE. WE NEED A REVOLUTION."

Eliza has always believed in standing up for zombie equality. While she was excited when zombies were invited to attend Seabrook High, she wasn't entirely surprised that we and our friends were sent to classes in the school basement. She had hoped to be treated as an equal, and even join the computer club, but progress for zombiekind was proving to be slow.

When I was recruited for the football team after I publicly (and accidentally) displayed my **zombie strength**, Eliza encouraged me to go out there and change things. She thought I could help **overthrow the system** by proving that zombies not only fit in but could help Seabrook thrive. She thought my success was a success for all zombies. First zombies were allowed to have lunch in the cafeteria. Who knew what could happen next? I felt pressure to succeed on the football field, so Eliza used her impressive computer skills to help me start hacking into my **Z-Band** to improve my zombie strength during games.

At first, Eliza didn't understand how I could like Addison. A cheerleader? **Really!** But as much as she tried to dislike her (she even called her Cheery McCheerstein), Eliza eventually realized that Addison was cool—not just for a human but actually **really cool**. She was Eliza's first human friend.

A TRUE ZOMBIE ADVOCATE

Eliza couldn't believe it when she heard that the town was planning to tear down the Seabrook Power Plant. It was an important landmark in the history of zombiekind, and she felt it needed to be preserved. Everyone else was excited about the new cheer pavilion that would stand in its place, but not Eliza. She campaigned to stop the demolition of this important building, but her efforts were for naught.

Later, when I was considering running for school president, Eliza was my biggest supporter. She thought that as a football star, I had already done so much for zombies. Imagine what I could do as school president! She felt like every **zombie success** was a step toward **zombie equality**. And she always makes it her mission to help her zombie friends succeed.

MEET ELIZA-BOT

During senior year, Eliza had an amazing opportunity to intern at Z-Tech, the creators of the Z-Band. We all missed her at Seabrook High, but we couldn't have been prouder. She was **thrilled** to be working at Z-Tech. There was so much to learn, and she was representing the zombie population with pride. "I literally broke the glass ceiling today . . . testing a prototype," she joked with me.

To help me and her other Seabrook friends feel like she was still there, Eliza made a **zom-punk robot** with spare parts she found around Z-Tech and sent it to Seabrook. It wasn't Eliza, but it was the next best thing!

Her robot double even had to stand in for her at Seabrook High's graduation. As the **first zombie valedictorian**, she had to represent!

MEET BONZO

- Artist, musician, DJ

- Member of the Mighty Shrimp cheer squad

- Afraid of fire

"ZARGARTEEKAWI" (TRANSLATION: LEAVING SEABROOK ISN'T THE END. IT'S THE BEGINNING!)

Bonzo is a zombie with **many talents**. He is a classically trained artist. He juggles, plays the tuba, is a sculptor of fruit and an origami expert, and likes to give hugs. He also speaks in his **native tongue: zombie**.

While he has many interests, Bonzo's favorite thing of all is being a **loyal** and **true friend** not just to me and Eliza, but to pretty much everyone he meets. He would do anything for his friends and knows we feel the same way about him.

CHEERING FOR CHANGE

Bonzo loved the positive vibes he got from the Mighty Shrimp cheer squad's routines. He wanted to be a part of bringing that joy to the crowds, so he decided to try out for the cheer squad and became one of the first **boundary-breaking zombies** on the championship team! (Also, he was excited to cheer for me on the field.)

During cheer practice, Bonzo got to know Addison's bestie, Bree. Her enthusiasm for cheer was off the charts. When he was around her, he couldn't help smiling. That was when he realized he was **crushing on a human**. And why not? Me and Addison were a great couple. They could follow in our footsteps. So Bonzo asked Bree to Prawn, and they've been together ever since!

ZOMBIE GOALS!

Bonzo may be a modern zombie, but he hasn't been able to shake one old-school zombie trait: he is **afraid of fire**. In fact, even though he loved going to his first pep rally, he was freaked out by the cheer squad's sparkly spirit sticks—so much so that he bolted from the stands and accidentally knocked over a few cheerleaders on the way.

And while Bonzo may be good at many things, he proved not to be a natural behind the wheel. He failed his first couple of **driver's license tests**, but in the end, he passed and can now drive Bree on proper dates.

MEET ZOEY

- Zed's little sister
- Aspiring cheerleader
- Dog lover

"I'M FIERCE! I DON'T KNOW WHAT YOU'RE UP TO, BIG BROTHER, BUT I'VE GOT YOUR BACK!"

Cheerleading, puppies, and hanging out with me, her devoted big brother, all make Zoey one happy zombie.

While going to football games to watch me play, Zoey discovered cheerleading and loved everything about it—from the cheer routines and pom-poms to the way cheerleaders like Bucky and Addison could excite the crowds. It was all so much fun to watch. She made up her own cheers and practiced them regularly, vowing to become the best cheerleader she could. She knew she was good, and she was confident that she would join the cheer squad when she grew up.

PUPPIES! PUPPIES! PUPPIES!

When she was younger, all Zoey ever wanted was **her own puppy**. Since zombies weren't allowed to have pets back then, she made do with her stuffed puppy, **Xander**, but she really wanted her own fluffy friend to take care of. I would sometimes pretend to be a puppy to amuse her. But that didn't stop her from dreaming of her very own puppy. Eventually, her wish came true, when Addison gifted her with a real dog.

GROWING INTO A ZOM-GIRL!

Zoey has always been my little sister, but she's not so little anymore. She really wanted to zombie out during the alien invasion, but I told her she was still too young for that. But when she went full zombie to help me protect Addison and the aliens, I couldn't have been prouder. **She's pretty fierce!**

WE ARE THE MIGHTY SHRIMP!

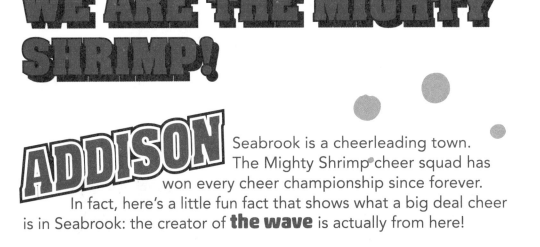

ADDISON

Seabrook is a cheerleading town. The Mighty Shrimp cheer squad has won every cheer championship since forever. In fact, here's a little fun fact that shows what a big deal cheer is in Seabrook: the creator of **the wave** is actually from here!

My grandmother, Angie, was one of the first members of the Mighty Shrimp cheer squad, back when it was just starting out. She loved everything about cheer—from choreographing and performing exciting cheer routines to **rallying fans** in the stands. Cheerleading became her passion, and the squad became like her family.

As the talented troop of cheerleaders began to gain recognition in cheer circles and earned awards, Seabrook started paying attention, too. Winning a spot on the squad became a big deal. If you were a Mighty Shrimp cheerleader, you were immediately accepted.

Later my mom, **Missy**, followed in her mom's footsteps and joined the squad. She helped them perfect their intricate routines and brought tumbling and gymnastics to the pep rally floor. My mom was a super-talented gymnast and her ability to top cheer pyramids was groundbreaking at the time. It's funny to think she was so free and open to trying anything back then. Now, as the **mayor of Seabrook**, she's pretty by the book and worries about what everyone thinks. She's still kind of freaked out about my white hair.

My cousin **Bucky** continued the family cheer tradition when he joined the squad. Say what you will about Bucky, but he's a pretty **amazing** cheerleader. He's a three-time MVP award winner, and I'm still in awe of how perfectly he lands his tumbling runs. Then there's me. I've always wanted to be a cheerleader, so I was thrilled when I made the team freshman year. While the squad had an award case

full of trophies, they still hadn't been able to rally the school's football team out of last place. From as far back as I could remember, our football team had struggled to find the end zone. But that all changed thanks to Zed. He began leading the team to victory. **The cheer squad finally had something to cheer about**. Seabrook had a winning football team and a championship cheer squad! It was like **a dream come true** for Seabrook High.

I was captain of the squad my senior year, which was amazing. I organized the National Cheer-Off and invited squads from all over to compete. I'm pretty proud of that. I will always love cheer, but I don't know if I'm going to join the squad at Mountain College yet. We'll see. A lot has changed since I figured out **who I really am**.

CHAMPIONS OF CHEER

When the **aliens arrived** in Seabrook for the National Cheer-Off, we were all a little surprised, but if you're going to travel across the galaxy for a cheer competition, why not come to Seabrook? I've always thought **cheer could unite people** from different walks of life, but this was more than I had hoped for.

The most coveted trophy in all of cheer is the **Seabrook Cup**. It's such a beautiful trophy it's almost otherworldly. My grandmother helped create this prized award, and she always loved this trophy in particular. When I found out it was constructed with materials from her planet, I understood why she cherished it so much. What could be more **precious** than an artifact from your home planet?

Bucky is almost as possessive of the Seabrook Cup as the werewolves are of their moonstone, so when he saw how **awesome** the aliens were at cheer, the possibility that they might win the cup at the National Cheer-Off and take it home with them—away from Seabrook—was really troubling to him.

He wasn't very welcoming to the aliens, and neither were the werewolves, who don't trust outsiders. But I thought it was exciting that cheerleaders from another planet had come to Seabrook. As captain of the cheer squad, I wanted them to enjoy their time here. After all, we were their hosts at the National Cheer-Off, and if we were gonna win, it would be because our squad loved each other, not because we hated anyone else. And the aliens' intergalactic cheer excellence made us work extra hard to live up to the Mighty Shrimps' champion reputation.

MEET THE CHEERLEADERS

MEET ADDISON

- Cheer captain

- Most impressive cheer move: triple hip-hop double-tuck Lindy

- Plans to go to Mountain College

"I'VE ALWAYS BELIEVED THAT CHEER CAN BRING PEOPLE TOGETHER. MAYBE IT CAN BRING WORLDS TOGETHER!"

I come from a family of cheerleaders, and ever since I was little, I've wanted to be a cheerleader, too. That's really all I've ever wanted. Every summer, my parents sent me to cheer camp, and I loved it. I dreamed that one day I would join the award-winning **Mighty Shrimp** cheer squad.

On my first day at Seabrook High, I realized I had been pretty sheltered. I was living the Seabrook dream of the perfect home, the perfect family . . . the perfect life. I mean, my mom is the mayor, and my dad is the chief of police. How much more perfect can you get? I had never met a zombie, but I had been taught to fear them. Then I met **Zed**, and I realized everything is not always what it appears to be.

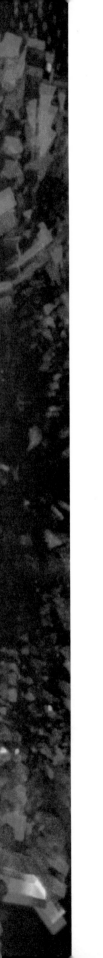

WHERE'S MY PACK?

I always thought I was a totally normal teen except for my silvery-white hair. It's some rare genetic disease. I can't dye it; no hair color will stick. My parents taught me that it was important to fit in at all costs, so we started hiding my mysterious hair under a wig when I was just a little girl. No one in Seabrook knew I was different, but my hair always made me feel like an outsider.

When I met Zed and realized that zombies were outsiders, too, I started to see that **being different was okay**. I took off my wig and began to wear my own hair with pride. But I still wondered who I was.

The werewolves thought that I might be one of their pack, and I was excited to think that I had found where I belonged. I went with them to their den in the Forbidden Forest and saw a real community. They knew who they were supposed to be, and they were a family. But unfortunately, there was no call to the wild for me.

Finally, when the aliens came to Seabrook and their mother ship accidentally beamed me up, I discovered my **true roots**. The ship had detected my **alien genes**, and I found out once I was on board that my grandmother was from their planet. My hair was supposed to glow with stardust sparkle, like the aliens', but I had been so far removed from my alien roots that **my hair lost its glow**.

The aliens wanted me to return with them to space to search for their **utopia**. My grandmother had hidden inside me—her most precious possession—the coordinates to a new home for her species. Because **the map** would recalibrate as we traveled, I needed to go with the aliens.

I was going to miss my family and friends in Seabrook. And most of all, I was going to miss Zed and our plan to go away together to Mountain College. But it seemed like my destiny to travel to space with my people.

In the end, we wound up back in Seabrook. It was the utopia my grandmother had discovered for her people. And once I knew I was one of her people, I couldn't agree more that **Seabrook was the perfect place to call home**. Humans, zombies, werewolves, aliens, and anyone else who arrived here would always be welcome.

I DON'T FEEL LIKE I BELONG

Until recently, I didn't know where I fit in. I didn't have a zombie crew or my own pack. I wanted to find out where I belonged, and then the aliens came to town and I discovered my **otherworldly heritage**. Now I finally know who I am!

While I was figuring it out, I tried a bunch of different looks. Right now **I'm rocking my blue-alien vibe**. Who knows what will come next?

When I finally revealed my white hair, everyone thought it was weird, but then they got used to it.

My parents were totally confused by my werewolf look. My dad asked if I had joined a rock band.

A little stardust sparkle transformed my high school cheerleader look into something otherworldly.

Once my alien genes were completely activated, I went for the full-on alien fashion statement!

CHEERFUL attitude

MEET
BUCKY

- Addison's cousin
- Former cheer captain
- School president

"PEOPLE LOVE ME! I'VE GOT JAZZ HANDS!"

As head of Seabrook High's award-winning cheer squad, my cousin **Bucky ruled the school**. I have to admit he's an amazing cheerleader, and he has always been supportive of my joining the squad. He can perform impressive tumble runs, is a big fan of jazz hands, and knows how to rock sequins. His loyal cheer squad included the Aceys (Stacey, Lacey, and Jacey . . . oh, and can't forget about Tracey), who would do anything for him.

Bucky, however, knew the power that came with being the captain of the Mighty Shrimp cheer squad, and he was pretty ruthless in maintaining control of the cheer spotlight. He believed in Seabrook's rule that **we can all keep winning if we just try to fit in**. He wanted the status quo in Seabrook to remain while he sat back and polished cheer trophies.

BUCKY FOR PRESIDENT

When Bucky got a taste of power as cheer captain, he decided to one-up that power and run for school president. He had visions of a corner office at school and being able still to rule the cheer squad.

"Great news. We have a brilliant and cheer-tested candidate running for president this year: me," he told the crowd when he announced his candidacy at school. His election slogan was very on-brand, too: A vote for Bucky is a vote for **cheer-fection**.

Zed tried to run against him, but Bucky played dirty. He hung up banners with pictures of Zed looking like a monster. And after Zed accidentally zombied out at an election rally, Bucky had the election won.

OUT OF THIS WORLD

Even though Bucky wasn't technically on the cheer squad anymore, he still showed up to all our events. I think he missed cheer . . . and the limelight. When the aliens arrived, Bucky felt it was his job to protect the Seabrook Cup, like it was his legacy and he didn't want it ever to leave Seabrook.

He also didn't want to face the fact that if Grandma Angie was actually an alien, there was some alien in his blood, too. That would make him different. "I'm not an alien," he proclaimed. "I'm an ordinary person. An extraordinarily normal spectacularly fabulous ordinary awesome person."

But in the end, he came to terms with his **alien heritage** and even decided to share his mastery of cheer with other galaxies. He bid Seabrook "sis boom buh-bye!" and headed out to space for **a cheer-tastic adventure**.

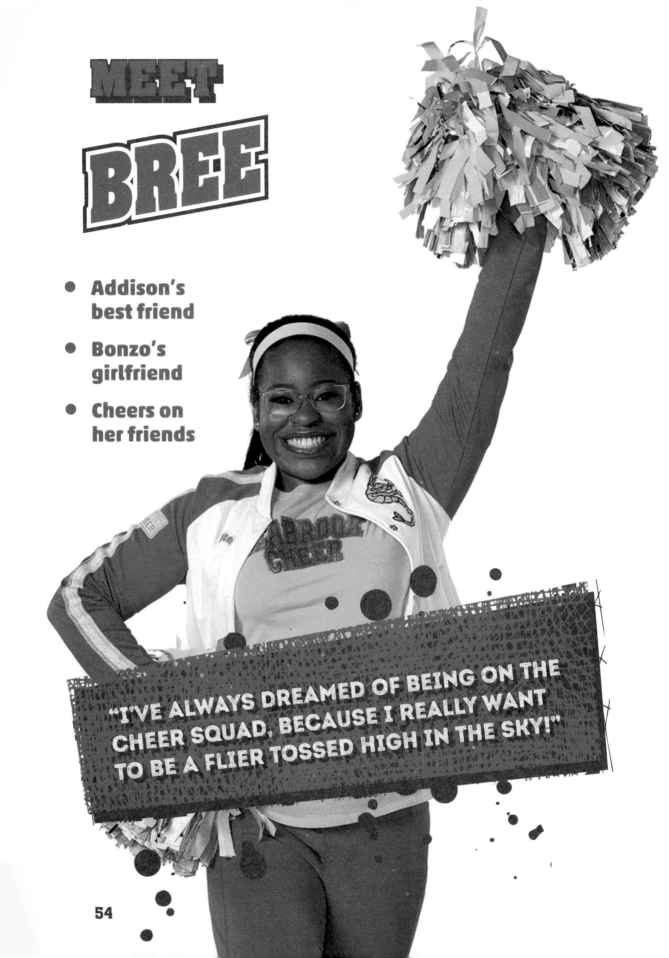

MEET
BREE

- Addison's best friend
- Bonzo's girlfriend
- Cheers on her friends

"I'VE ALWAYS DREAMED OF BEING ON THE CHEER SQUAD, BECAUSE I REALLY WANT TO BE A FLIER TOSSED HIGH IN THE SKY!"

When I met Bree on our first day at Seabrook High, I knew right away that we were gonna be friends. Naturally bubbly and incredibly positive, Bree was made to be a cheerleader. We tried out for cheer together. I'm so glad she made the squad even though Bucky thought she should start as an alternate. I can't imagine cheer without her.

The first day, Bucky and the Aceys drove Bree and me to Zombietown for **cheer initiation**. "We like to remind zombies that we don't accept freaks in this town," Bucky told us. He handed us a carton of eggs and drove off, leaving two girls alone in the unfamiliar community. We had never been to Zombietown before and had no idea what life was like for zombies. Were they always harassed like this?

I had **just met Zed** earlier that day, and there he was, coming out of his house. He saw Bree and me huddled in the corner with our carton of eggs, and you could tell from the look in his eyes that he was so disappointed in us. It was awful. I've never felt worse.

A LOYAL FRIEND

Bree isn't just an amazing cheerleader—she's **a true and loyal friend**. She could tell I liked Zed, and she was so supportive. "I have your back no matter what," she said. "I just don't want him to break your heart . . . or eat it."

Later Bucky told me I had to choose between Zed and cheer. I chose cheer, but when I decided to lead a cheer for Zed on the field, Bucky threatened to kick me off the squad. Bree joined my cheer in a show of solidarity, and Bucky kicked us both off the squad.

That's just one of the many times Bree has been there for me. When she thought I had been kidnapped by werewolves, she came with our friends into the Forbidden Forest to save me, even though I didn't need saving. And when I didn't transform into a werewolf after I put on a moonstone necklace, Bree was there to comfort me. "You're beautiful, Addie, but the same kind of beautiful you've always been," she said.

I know how lucky I am to have Bree as a friend. I'm going to miss her when I go away to school, but I know **we'll always stay in touch**.

BREE HEARTS BONZO

I'm not the only cheerleader to have a zombie boyfriend. Bree had a crush on Zed's friend Bonzo, and after he joined the cheer squad, he realized how amazing Bree is, too.

He asked her to Prawn, and they've been together ever since. She always has a big smile on her face when he's around. They are pretty much **adorable**.

I think we are all really excited that high school is over, but for Bree and Bonzo, it's a little bittersweet. I remember her telling Bonzo, "I wish we could be cheerleaders forever. Maybe we should flunk science so high school never ends. Nah, we have too much chemistry!"

How cute is that!

BE FEARLESS, NOT CHEERLESS!

"Cheer until it hurts" is one of Bucky's favorite expressions, and his squad of assistant captains—Stacey, Lacey, and Jacey (and Tracey), also known as the **Aceys**—was willing to do anything to make sure cheer stayed in the spotlight. The Aceys have always followed every last one of Bucky's directions, even after he left cheer to be school president. You could say they were his co-conspirators.

Bucky believed at first that zombies distracted people from what's really important: cheer! "Cheer is being threatened. Are you ready to protect it?" he told the squad. He even went on to kick off the squad

cheerleaders who showed any sort of loyalty toward zombies. Needless to say, Bree and I got booted almost immediately.

But when the minimal squad couldn't pull it together for the cheer championship that year, it was Zoey and a group of zombies who helped them come together and shine at the event. Bonzo had so much fun at that competition he even went on to join the squad.

At cheer camp the following year, the Aceys were still ensuring Bucky's reign. But Bucky had lightened up on the zombies a little. He was starting to see that maybe they could help the squad. He also invited Bree and me to return to the squad. The Aceys pulled my letters to Zed out of the mail while I was at camp and shredded them. It was like they wanted to make sure what happened at cheer camp stayed at cheer camp. "Once we are co–cheer captains, you're so off the team," Stacey and Lacey said to me. I think they were just feeling threatened because they could see that things were changing. Zombies were on the squad, and **cheer was bringing people together**. That's what I always thought cheer could do.

So what does the future hold for the Mighty Shrimp cheer squad? When I go to Mountain College, I'm leaving the squad in good hands. There are a couple of cheerleaders who could be great captains. And who knows? When Zoey gets to Seabrook High, maybe she'll end up being the **first zombie cheer captain**! She definitely has the talent.

WE OWN THE NIGHT

WILLA Werewolves have lived in the Forbidden Forest since the early days of Seabrook. It is our home. Our pack was living in Seabrook long before the first human settlers arrived. They thought we were wild beasts and drove us deep into the Forbidden Forest, where we built a community of wolves that live together like **one big family**.

Those early settlers discovered our **moonstone** and stole it for themselves. I've looked through the history books in the Seabrook High library, and they are filled with lies. There's no mention of how the humans took our **precious energy source** from us.

Everyone in our pack wears a moonstone necklace, and our moonstones make us our **true werewolf selves**. Without them, we'd die. But those necklaces have to be charged every hundred years by the moonstone for us to stay wolf strong.

Legend had it that a great alpha would appear and lead us to our moonstone. The **white-haired leader** we had been promised looked a lot like Addison, so when she appeared in the Forbidden Forest after her cheerleading bus crashed off the road, Wyatt thought the Great Alpha had arrived. I wasn't so sure, but if so, it wasn't a moment too soon. Members of our pack were already starting to get sick as their moonstone necklaces lost their charges. We needed the Great Alpha to help us find our moonstone right away!

Werewolves aren't afraid of a lot—well, silver, ticks, and rabies aren't our favorite things—but we all fear losing the power that our moonstone necklaces provide. The glowing stone charges our wolf strength more than any full moon.

While Addison didn't turn out to be the Great Alpha, she has been a **true friend** to the werewolf community. She helped rally Seabrook to find our moonstone, and for that we will be forever grateful. Wolves always have each other's backs. **And Addison is part of our pack. Forever.**

Today our moonstone resides on **Moonstone Circle** in the middle of Zombietown and is protected by a shimmery force field. **It's a symbol of strength and unity**, not just for werewolves but for everyone in Seabrook.

MEET THE
WEREWOLVES

MEET WILLA

- Head werewolf
- Lone wolf
- Protector of the moonstone

"I DON'T TRUST THE ALIENS. LAST TIME OUTSIDERS SWOOPED INTO SEABROOK, OUR MOONSTONE WAS STOLEN."

I'm a fierce, **proud werewolf**, but not everyone understands that. People think I'm angry, but I'm just very guarded. I feel responsible for protecting my werewolf family. **No one is going to mess with my pack.**

Sure, I might have some trust issues, but look at werewolf history. We've been driven from our land and repeatedly lied to, and we've had our most valuable possession stolen. And people say we're monsters! So, yeah, **you have to earn my trust**.

I thought Seabrook was horrible at first, and I just wanted to find our moonstone so we could go back to living in the **Forbidden Forest**. I didn't trust Zed and Addison, either, but now I do. They went out of their way to help the wolves and showed us that **together we can do anything**. I didn't trust the aliens when they arrived in Seabrook, but I'm starting to. . . .

HOWLING WITH HOPE

Addison welcomed the werewolves to Seabrook immediately. And when we asked her to come with us into the Forbidden Forest, she didn't hesitate. Maybe that's why we really thought she was the Great Alpha.

We gave Addison a fully charged **moonstone necklace**, and if she was truly one of us, she would have turned into a werewolf when she put it on. She wanted to think about it for a day. When I found out she had lost this prized werewolf artifact, I was so mad and I knew she wasn't who we had thought she was. The Great Alpha would never lose something so valuable. She would guard it with her life.

But even though she made a mistake, Addison came through for us. She came to the Seabrook Power Plant and tried to stop its demolition so we could look for our moonstone. She knew how important it was to us and didn't want to see it get crushed under the rubble of the historic plant.

DON'T LIE TO ME

There's nothing I hate more than being lied to. We kind of knew something was going on before the aliens arrived in Seabrook, because our moonstones started acting up. When the aliens showed up, they weren't honest about their reason for visiting. I mean, who would travel all that way for a cheer competition? If they had just told us they were looking for their scout ship, I would have appreciated that, and our pack could have helped them.

Then the fact that Addison and Zed knew the aliens' secret and didn't tell me or the other werewolves just made me **howling mad**. What else were they not sharing with me? But in the end, I have to trust Zed and Addison, and even A-spen and the aliens. I know Addison is like a member of our pack, and she and Zed had their reasons for not letting me in on their plans. I'm so used to being a **lone wolf** I'm not used to trusting anyone . . . not even my friends. That's something I have to work on!

MEET WYATT

- Willa's brother
- Has a crush on Eliza
- Fro-yo lover

"WEREWOLVES ARE A PART OF SEABROOK, TOO. THE ORIGINALS, IN FACT."

Wyatt is my brother and likes to think he is in charge of the pack. News flash: he's not! He's **too trusting** and too **easily distracted** to be a good leader.

After we saw Addison in the Forbidden Forest, Wyatt went into Seabrook to see what he could find out about her. He dressed like a Seabrook Power Plant worker and sniffed around town. We knew Addison went to Seabrook High, so we all decided to go into town and find her. I guess I didn't really think through our plan, because when we showed up at Seabrook High to take Addison, everyone kind of **freaked out**.

"We can't go to war with the whole town. We'll never find the moonstone if they're on high alert," Wyatt told me. I hate it when he's right. So we enrolled at Seabrook High. After all, the Forbidden Forest is in the school district. Then we got to know Addison, to see if she was the **Great Alpha**.

Wyatt liked her right away. He also couldn't stop talking about something called **fro-yo**. See what I mean about being easily distracted?

THE HUNT FOR THE MOONSTONE

Wyatt was busy practicing cheerleading, eating fro-yo, and making new friends in Seabrook. He knew how important it was to find the moonstone, but he didn't seem to realize the urgency. He was enjoying life outside the Forbidden Forest for the first time, and he was sure Addison would lead us to what we were looking for.

And she did, in a way. She thought the moonstone might be hidden in **Seabrook Power Plant**, and Wyatt was sure she was right, so the pack made its way to the soon-to-be-demolished building to look around. Unfortunately, we got detained by the Z-Patrol, and even though Zed and Addison were able to halt the demolition, something went wrong, and the plant was destroyed. We thought we'd never find our moonstone under the pile of rubble.

Later, at the Prawn dance, the ground rumbled and a fault line opened up the earth, revealing **underground tunnels**. We went down into them to look for our moonstone. "Legend says that together we can move the moonstone," Wyatt told us, but when we found it in an underground chamber, it wouldn't budge.

"Well, maybe you need to expand your pack," Addison said as she arrived with a group of zombies and cheerleaders to help us move our moonstone to safety. I've never been more relieved . . . and grateful. But again, I hate it when Wyatt is right!

TECH WOLF

Wyatt is pretty **tech savvy**. Maybe that's why he has a thing for Eliza. The two of them like to **geek out** about all things electronic.

It's kind of funny, though, that when Eliza was gone at her internship at Z-Tech, Wyatt was always trying to talk to her **Z-Bot** here in Seabrook. I guess it made him feel like he was spending time with her, even though it was a robot. But his moonstone necklace kept shorting out the Z-Bot screen. Wyatt knows our moonstone necklaces can zap out electronics, but he just kept doing it and acting surprised every time. I guess he's not thinking straight when he's around even a robot version of Eliza!

MEET
WYNTER

- Football girl
- Likes cat videos
- Loves being scratched behind her ears

"I HOWL AT THE MOON TO LET OUT TENSION. SOMETIMES IT'S NOT EVEN A FULL MOON. SOMETIMES IT'S THE SUN."

Wynter thinks she's tough, but she's like a wolf pup. She's **totally innocent** and needs to be **protected** from enemies of our pack.

When we left the Forbidden Forest to go into Seabrook to look for the moonstone and charge our necklaces, it was Wynter's first time out of the den. She tried to be fierce, but she couldn't hide how excited she was to see what the rest of the world was like. That didn't stop her from talking tough. She was the first to proclaim that we were **mean and rough beasts** of the forest and could never be tamed. Then Zed's little sister, Zoey, scratched her behind the ear, and she turned into a **big fluffy puppy**.

Later, when her moonstone powers started to fade and she started getting sick, it was hard to watch her lose her energy. I'm used to her having a bounce in her step, and I did not like seeing her so **listless**. After all, it's my job to look out for her and the rest of the pack.

WILD style

GROOMED TO IMPRESS

Werewolves know hair and nails, but Wynter is probably the **most stylish werewolf** in our pack. She's always got a new hairstyle and wears cool outfits. And she's all about getting manicures.

FIERCE AT FOOTBALL

Zed saw how fierce Wynter wanted to be, so he offered to teach her to tackle. Later she went to her first football game at Seabrook High and knew she had to try out for the team. Something about being allowed to go a little wild on the football field really appealed to her. It didn't intimidate her that everyone else on the field was male. She just wanted to get out there and **play the game**.

Wynter likes to **talk tough**, even though she's actually **really sweet**. My favorite rant of hers was "Our razor-sharp claws will gut them and splatter their blood." Even she knew that was a little too much!

ALIEN INVASION

A-SPEN We were sent to Seabrook from a distant galaxy to find our **missing scout ship** that landed here sixty-five years ago. The scout was in search of a **new Utopia** for our people, but when her spaceship ran out of fuel and crashed, she couldn't return home to share her findings. Instead, she lived out her life in Seabrook . . . with humans. Seabrook never knew an alien had been living among them until we arrived.

Our journey was difficult. To get here, we developed interstellar flight, defeated space squids, and traversed a carnivorous black hole . . . twice. Space squids are worthy adversaries. Not only do they fight with many arms, but space squids also shoot black ink, which covered Mothership's windows, making it impossible to see what lay ahead. Luckily, our advanced navigational tools allowed us to find our way.

We had come to Seabrook in peace. We just wanted to recover the scout's log. Our people needed a **new home**, since our planet had been destroyed by environmental blight built up over years. No one spoke out while our planet was suffering—all because we didn't want to create disharmony. Looking back now, that seems unfortunate. Conflict isn't always bad. **Being challenged sometimes pushes us to be better.**

Seabrook residents were surprised by our arrival. We didn't want to scare the local citizens, so when we saw a flyer for the **National Cheer-Off**, we told them we had come to take part in this important competition. And they believed us! We didn't even know what cheer was.

THE POWER OF STARDUST

Stardust is an integral part of alien life. We generate stardust electricity through special gloves we wear. That powerful electricity is **invaluable**. For example, when we found our scout ship, one zap of stardust electricity was able to activate a long-dormant projector so we could access a hologram of the scout's log.

Our gloves are also embedded with a powerful removable **luma lens**. A luma lens can be used as a **mind probe** so we can view others' memories. It can also be used to levitate objects. Alien tech is far more advanced than Earth technology. We have found Seabrook to have far less superior technology.

We are telepaths and communicate by reading each other's minds. In Seabrook, the residents talk . . . a lot. And they have so many feelings. We **value peace**, so we have emotional suppressors. Emotions can get messy for telepaths, so we suppress them . . . but they do seem interesting.

I decided to turn off my **emotion suppressor** to try to understand these humans. It was so exciting . . . and that was my first emotion: **excitement**.

SCOUT REPORT

When we **found our scout ship**, the scout's log was partially corrupt. We got the file back to the mother ship, where we were able to recover it:

This is Scout Commander 15-09. I proudly report my mission is complete. For centuries, we have been without a home. But I found Utopia—the perfect new planet for our people. I hid the coordinates in the most precious thing in Seabrook. You must find the most precious thing in Seabrook.

Many decades ago, out of fuel, my scout ship crashed on this planet. I would've died if not for a young humanoid, Eli. He hid me and nursed me back to health. But with no ship to take me home, I was forced to hide my true identity.

I joined Eli in his school and discovered my passion: cheerleading. I even created a trophy.

But while I was no longer in contact with our people, my hair grew white and I lost my stardust powers. Though I gained something else: a family. Eli and I fell in love and married. And we named our firstborn A-Mishanta. But we always called her Missy.

When the hologram of the scout took off her helmet, it was revealed that she was **Addison's grandma Angie**. Addison was thrilled. She finally knew why her hair was white and who she really was.

Addison's **hair strobed blue** when she first came into contact with her grandmother's luma lens, but the stardust electricity didn't interact with her. "Our relationship with stardust defines us," I told her. "Our technology will not work for you. Sorry. You do not have our spark. **You are not truly one of us.**"

She seemed very sad. Again, emotions can be messy!

WHERE IS OUR MAP?

We needed to find the most precious thing in Seabrook if we were going to find the **map to Utopia** for our people. Zed agreed to help us if we helped him with his application to Mountain College. We are shrewd negotiators, but this seemed a fair deal.

We first checked the moonstone. The moonstone's crystal formation has the processing power to hold our map's coordinates. Zed warned us that the werewolves wouldn't let outsiders near the moonstone. He was right. A-lan discovered the moonstone was protected by an invisible force field when he tried to get near it. He got a giant **ZAP!** We took the force field down with our stardust electricity. Unfortunately, the coordinates were not there. Mission failed.

Our next thought was the map might be in the Seabrook Cup. The trophy was created by our scout and constructed with materials from our planet. What could be more precious than an artifact from our home world? We thought the map had to be there, and we had to win the trophy in the National Cheer-Off to get it. But we discovered we were wrong again. Mission failed.

We finally discovered our map coordinates were within Addison. She was the **most precious thing** in Seabrook to her grandmother. Unfortunately, the map to Utopia was dynamic, constantly computing new inputs to guide our spaceship. So Addison needed to come with us to Utopia. Lucky for us, she agreed to join us in space, even though it meant leaving her friends and family behind in Seabrook. Zed wanted to come, too, but only aliens can survive space travel.

LOOK! UP IN THE SKY!

We arrived in Seabrook the night of something called a **big championship game**. We weren't sure what that was, but apparently it's a really important event in Seabrook. The sky filled with ominous **supernatural clouds**, and when Mothership emerged from them, Seabrook thought they were under attack. We beamed down to the ground and left Mothership in the sky. Mothership is where we have been living since our planet was destroyed.

When Addison and Zed came on board to visit, Addison recognized our script on the walls. She remembered herself and her grandmother using it in secret code games when she was a child. Even though she hadn't known at the time that her grandmother was an alien, some of Addison's first memories are alien-centric.

When our new friends arrived on the bridge, they seemed pretty impressed. It is like an alien tech wonderland for humans. I felt very proud to share it with them. Oh, I believe that was another emotion I was able to experience for the first time!

But Mothership is a spaceship. She is not our home. We found our Utopia. It's called Seabrook.

MEET
A-SPEN

- Leader of the aliens
- Excited to experience emotions
- Favorite fro-yo flavor: chocolate

"HARMONY ISN'T SILENCE. UNITY ISN'T SAMENESS. LOVE IS POWERFUL. IT CAN HANDLE DISAGREEMENT. AND SO MUST UTOPIA."

Space travel can be exhausting. When we finally arrived in Seabrook, we were all tired and space-lagged. We just wanted to find our scout ship and scout's log. But it turned out there was much to discover in Seabrook.

We weren't impressed by humans at first, but we found there was much we could learn from them. When I turned off my emotional suppressor, it was the **first time I experienced emotions**. Sure, conflict and sadness are hard emotions to go through, but then there was **joy**, **love**, and **admiration**—messy, but definitely worth experiencing!

We made new friends, who helped us find our map to Utopia and fix Mothership when we needed to return to space. We even met a few new aliens—Addison, Missy, and Bucky—which was unexpected.

IS THIS LOVE?

Emotions can be so confusing. I had feelings I couldn't define. One day, my palms were sweaty and it felt like space moths were in my stomach. Was I sick? Did I have the space flu? I asked Addison, and she got excited. "I think you have a crush!" she said. "It's like when you connect with someone in a strong way."

I told her I had a somewhat irrational desire to be with someone, and she assured me I was experiencing **my first crush**. When I told her my crush was on Zed, she seemed surprised at first, but then she told me that she also loved Zed and that they were a couple. I tried to understand. One must have a crush only on someone who is not part of a couple? One must control who one loves?

In the end, our love was too complicated, so I had to break up with Zed. He seemed confused. I think I mastered human relationships. I told him, though, we'd always have the invasion!

Later, I found someone better for me, someone with passion! Who knew I'd be so taken with a werewolf! When I first met Willa, Zed warned me to be careful of my heart. But I wasn't worried. She was like no one I had ever met before.

I told Willa that the stars shined so much brighter when I was sharing them with her. **And stars are a big deal to me!**

MEET A-LAN

- Competitive
- Good at all sports
- Favorite fro-yo flavor: chocolate

"THE JOY OF COMPETITION HAS CONSUMED ME. AND UNFORTUNATELY, I'M SO GOOD AT WINNING."

When we arrived in Seabrook and the Z-Patrol took us into custody, they showed A-lan to a holding room and put him in shackles. He didn't understand why he was being left alone in this new place. He quickly undid what he thought was some form of ceremonial jewelry, rewired the door panel to open, and went to look for the others.

"May you find harmony," he said, greeting the humans. I think they were surprised by how easy it had been for him to escape. It was their first glimpse at our advanced race.

Then, when we went to Seabrook High, our **superior education** made it possible for us to blow through the school's coursework. We even completed an entire year of one class in twenty-three minutes. We might have completed the work sooner if we could have figured out the electric pencil sharpener. What a superior writing instrument the pencil is!

THE THRILL OF VICTORY

One of the new things A-lan discovered in Seabrook was the **thrill of competition**. He loved it. "We are harmonious people. We do not compete amongst ourselves . . . but it is an intriguing concept," he said at first. But once he tried competing, he found being better than others was very enjoyable.

Zed is Seabrook's exceptional athlete, but A-lan far exceeds his sporting skills. A-lan broke many athletic records, like the most weights lifted in a bench press. This made Zed sad (again with the messy emotions). The humans said A-lan was a **VIFO** (Very Identifiable Flying Object) when he ruled the high jump event—another record he put his name on.

Zed was very forgiving about the breaking of his records. He helped us find our map, and in return, we helped him with his college application. It seemed very important to him, so we found an Exceptional Student scholarship he was eligible for at Mountain College. We didn't think he was exceptional at first, but now that we know him, we can see that he is!

When we gathered to practice for the National Cheer-Off, it became obvious that we were the far superior cheerleaders. Just the idea of winning the competition thrilled A-lan. He even learned to talk trash.

MEET A-LI

- Experiencing harmony and hostility

- Not a fan of Earth

- Favorite fro-yo flavor: mint chip

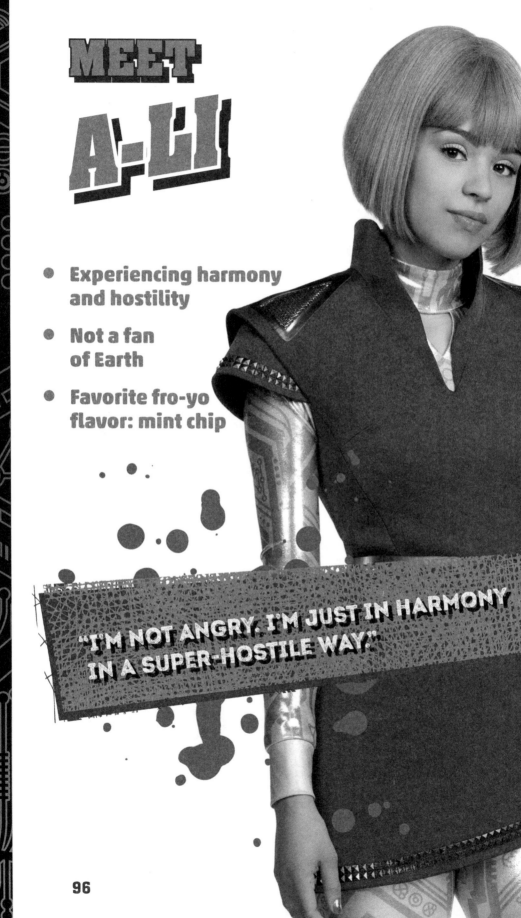

"I'M NOT ANGRY. I'M JUST IN HARMONY IN A SUPER-HOSTILE WAY."

A-li was ready to leave Seabrook the minute we arrived. Maybe all that time traveling through space had made her irritable. And that's with her emotion suppressor still activated. She was even annoyed when the residents of Seabrook thought they were under attack when we arrived. "We do not want your one-star planet," she told them.

She was finding it hard to remain "one people, in harmony, at any cost" on Earth. We all were, I guess. I was enjoying emotions, A-lan discovered competition, and A-li just needed off this planet. We were worried she might accidentally vaporize someone or something if she didn't leave Earth soon.

WHEN CHEER BECOMES AGGRESSIVE . . .

While we did not know what cheer was when we first came to Seabrook, Addison was very welcoming and taught us about this spirited pastime. Our **telepathic groupthink** made cheer so easy for us. And we could use our luma lenses for levitation. A-lan was excited by this, because he enjoyed winning. A-li was just annoyed. She thought that we were so far superior to the Mighty Shrimp cheer squad that competition wasn't worthy of our time.

SEABROOK HIGH SCHOOL · SQUILLA FORTI SEMPER

Even A-li had to admit, however, that Seabrook possessed one superior thing: fro-yo. The town's creamy dessert is out of this world and a great source of happiness for her.

In the end, she found cheer a common perspective with humans. I hope she will find harmony through cheer now that we have found **a new home in Seabrook**.

SEABROOK
UNITED

LOST IN SPACE?

ZED Everyone was sad when Addison said she would be leaving Seabrook with the aliens—especially me. She felt it was **her destiny** to help her people, and because the map coordinates to the aliens' new home were stored within her, she needed to travel with them so they could find it. "This is the hardest decision I've ever made, but I have to **do what is right**," she said. I got that. I thought I could just go with her, but unfortunately zombies cannot survive space travel.

Before the aliens could leave, though, they had to repair their mother ship, which had been damaged by the power of the werewolves' moonstone necklaces. They estimated that there

was only a 67.9 percent chance the spaceship could return to space, unless its power source was restored. Everyone in Seabrook joined together to help. The werewolves brought their moonstone to recharge the spaceship, and Eliza and Wyatt worked together to figure out how to channel the moonstone's power into the ship. Then Addison and I served as the conduits to transfer the power, which was kind of intense.

It all happened so fast, and before we knew it, the aliens and Addison were gone. I thought I would never see Addison again. I had been afraid we'd be separated by a couple hundred miles when she went to college. But we were gonna be separated by galaxies. It didn't matter how far away we were from each other; **we'd always be together**. But it was still a total bummer.

SOMEDAY, SOMEDAY . . .

ZED When Addison ventured off to space, she really left a void in Seabrook. She was the **unifying voice** that brought us all together. She was the first person to **accept everyone**, no matter whether they were a zombie, a werewolf, or an alien. She didn't see differences. She just saw the importance of welcoming each and every person, no matter who they were. Because of her, **no one in Seabrook ever has to feel alone**.

"No matter how far away she goes, she'll always be a part of our pack," Willa said, but you could tell she was really gonna miss Addison.

As for me, I can't even begin to express how much **I would miss Addison**!

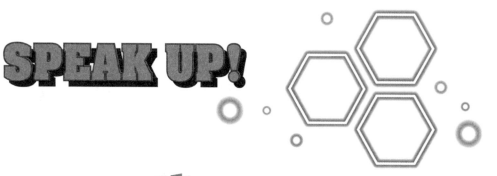

SPEAK UP!

A-SPEN After we left Seabrook to find our Utopia, we realized we would really miss the people of Seabrook. When we had first arrived to find our scout ship, we hoped Seabrook residents would take the opportunity to learn from our advanced intelligence, but in the end, it was us who learned from them.

No one had spoken up while our planet suffered. In Seabrook, we learned that **harmony isn't silence**. Once we overcame our initial discord with the people of Seabrook, we all became friends. Everyone in town rallied to help us fix our ship so we could return to space, even after we were dishonest about our real reason for visiting Seabrook in the first place.

When we were able to return to space, A-li wondered why our original scout, Addison's grandmother, hadn't just revealed the coordinates of Utopia in her scout report. Why had she sent us on a hunt for the missing map? "Maybe she thought there was something to be learned by staying in Seabrook for a while," Addison pondered aloud. That gave us all something to really think about.

"Mothership is a marvelous ship, but it is not our home," A-lan said. **I believe we found our Utopia—our home—in Seabrook.**

SEABROOK IS WHERE I BELONG!

ADDISON Space travel made me realize how much I missed everyone and everything about Seabrook. **I have so many wonderful memories here.**

GRADUATION DAY

 Addison was the first person to really see me, Willa . . . all of us, so her absence on graduation day at Seabrook High was felt by everyone. What should have been a day of joy and excitement about the future felt bittersweet. We were all so busy thinking about what came next that we almost missed a streak in the sky as Mothership returned to Seabrook. Then Addison and the aliens beamed down from it.

"You thought I was going to let intergalactic space travel get in the way of graduating?" Addison joked. She told us she and the aliens were here to stay. **Best graduation present ever!**

TO THE END OF THE UNIVERSE

ADDISON What do I think will happen when Zed and I go away to Mountain College together? We're gonna be fine, just fine. **Ain't no doubt about it!**

ZED I was super excited to learn that Mountain College is inviting other monsters to apply, too. Monsters won't need to pretend they fit in anymore, because we don't. We take pride in that. **It's okay to be different.**

As for me and Addison, I would love her to the end of the universe. But Mountain College seems a whole lot closer.